# Practise Your Phonics With
# Julia Donaldson's
# Songbirds

OXFORD
UNIVERSITY PRESS

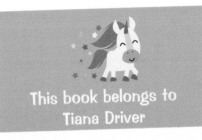

This book belongs to
Tiana Driver

# OXFORD
## UNIVERSITY PRESS

Great Clarendon Street, Oxford, OX2 6DP, United Kingdom

Oxford University Press is a department of the University of Oxford.
It furthers the University's objective of excellence in research, scholarship
and education by publishing worldwide. Oxford is a registered trade mark
of Oxford University Press in the UK and in certain other countries

Text © Julia Donaldson 2007
*The Red Man and the Green Man* illustrations © Andy Parker 2007
*Pirates* illustrations © Matt Buckingham 2007
*Tails* illustrations © Carol Liddiment 2007
*Pen-Pals* illustrations © Alison Bartlett 2007
*My Cat* illustrations © Barbara Vagnozzi 2007
*Tim's Bad Mood* illustrations © Andy Hammond 2007

The moral rights of the author have been asserted

First Edition published 2007
This Edition published 2012

British Library Cataloguing in Publication Data
Data available

978-0-19-279302-7

10 9

Printed in China

Paper used in the production of this book is a natural, recyclable product
made from wood grown in sustainable forests. The manufacturing process
conforms to the environmental regulations of the country of origin.

**Acknowledgements**
Series editor Clare Kirtley

Helping your child's learning
with free eBooks, essential
tips and fun activities
**www.oxfordowl.co.uk**

# Songbirds

# The Red Man and the Green Man

Story by Julia Donaldson
Pictures by Andy Parker
Series editor Clare Kirtley

OXFORD
UNIVERSITY PRESS

3

# Tips for reading The Red Man and the Green Man together

This book practises these letter patterns:

ee  ea  e  y  (all pronounced *ee* as in *three*)

ie  i-e  igh  i  (all pronounced *ie* as in *tie*)

oa  ow  o-e  o  (all pronounced *oe* as in *toe*)

ai  ay  a-e  a  (all pronounced *ai* as in *train*)

Ask your child to point to these letter patterns and say the sounds (e.g. *ie* as in *cries*). Look out for these letter patterns in the story.

Your child might find these words tricky:

of  into  to  the  are  they  all  live  people  these  says

one  two  goes  have  some  roll  here  do  what

These words are common, but your child may not be able to sound them out yet. Say the words for your child if they do not know them.

Before you begin, ask your child to read the title. Remind your child to read words they do not recognise by sounding out and blending. Look at the picture together. What do you think this story is about?

When you have finished reading the story, look through it again and:

- Ask your child, *Why didn't the red man and the green man enjoy their holiday?* (Because no one did what they told them to do.)
- Find and read some words on pages 19 and 20 which contain a long *ie* sound (*lights, seaside, right*). Point to the letter patterns that make the long *ie* vowel sound (*igh, i-consonant-e, igh*).

The red man and the green
man live inside the traffic lights.

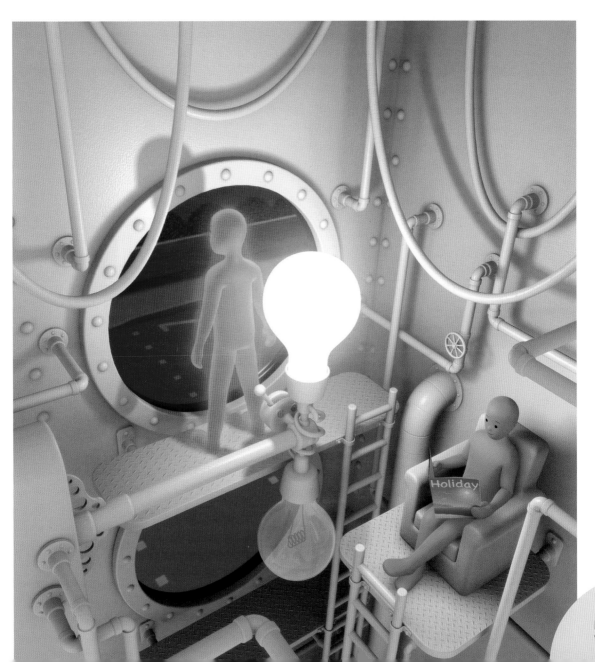

When people see the red man, they stop. When people see the green man, they can cross the road.

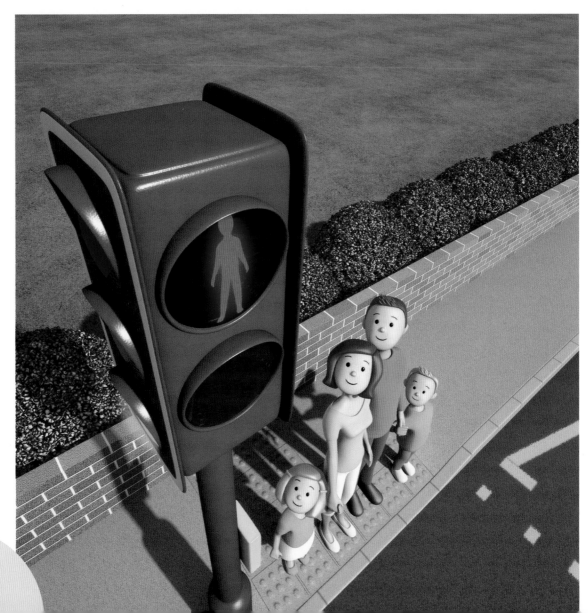

"I'm sick of these traffic lights," the red man says one day.
"So am I," says the green man.
"Let's go on holiday."

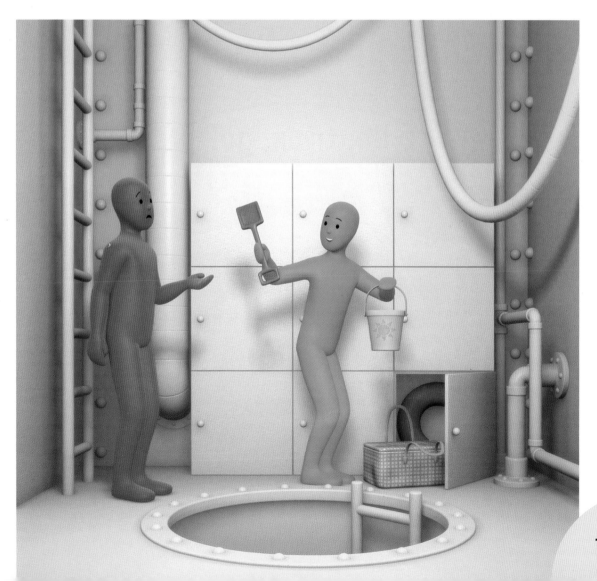

The red man and the green man get on a train. "Go, train, go," says the green man. But the train stays still.

In the end the train goes. The red man and the green man have a cup of tea.

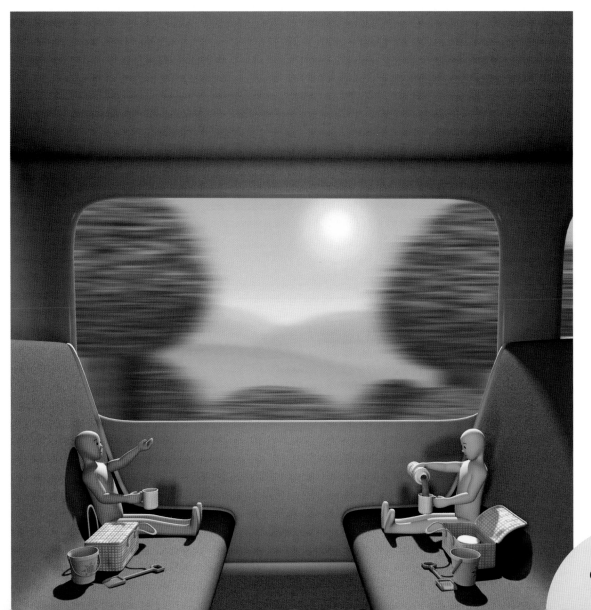

The red man sees the sea. "Stop, train, stop!" he cries. But the train keeps going.

In the end the train stops. The red man and the green man get off.

The two men go to the beach.
They make some traffic lights in
the sand.

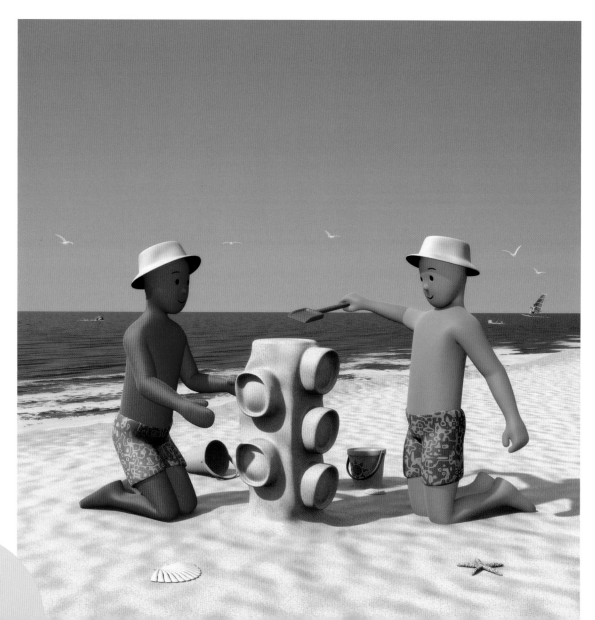

But then the waves roll in.
"Stop, waves, stop!" cries the red
man. But the waves don't stop.

They see a sea snail. It is sitting on a rock.

"Go, snail, go!" says the green man. But the snail stays still.

"No one stops when I tell them," says the red man.
"And no one goes when I tell them," says the green man.
"Let's go home."

The red man and the green man go back on the train.

Back home, no one knows when to cross the road. They are happy to see the red man and the green man again.

The two men hop up into the traffic lights.

"The seaside is all right, but here people do what we tell them," they say.

# Songbirds

# Pirates

Story by Julia Donaldson
Pictures by Matt Buckingham
Series Editor Clare Kirtley

**OXFORD**
UNIVERSITY PRESS

# Tips for reading Pirates together

This book practises these letter patterns:

> ee  ea  e  y  (all pronounced *ee* as in *three*)
>
> ie  i-e  igh  i  y  (all pronounced *ie* as in *tie*)
>
> oa  ow  o-e  o  (all pronounced *oe* as in *toe*)
>
> ai  ay  a-e  a  (all pronounced *ai* as in *train*)

Ask your child to point to these letter patterns and say the sounds (e.g. *y* as in *shy*). Look out for these letter patterns in the story.

Your child might find these words tricky:

> to  the  of  you  they  for  pirate  comes  have  we've  want

These words are common, but your child may not be able to sound them out yet. Say the words for your child if they do not know them.

Before you begin, ask your child to read the title. Remind your child to read words they do not recognise by sounding out and blending. Look at the picture together. What do you think this story is about?

When you have finished reading the story, look through it again and:

- Ask your child, *Why didn't Jack and Jade fight?* (They were too hot, then too hungry. Finally they became friends.)
- Find and read some words on page 37 which contain a long *ie* sound (*shy, I, write, I'll*). Point to the letter patterns that make the long vowel sound (*y, i, i-consonant-e, I*). Find and read some words on page 16 which contain a long *ai* sound (*Jade, wave, they, sail, away*).

Jack is a pirate. He is digging for gold.

Jack digs a deep hole.

While Jack is asleep, along comes
Pirate Jade.

Jade begins to dig in Jack's hole.

She digs up a chest and opens the lid.

Jack wakes up and sees Jade.

29

Jack and Jade have a swim.
They splash and play.

31

Jade catches a fish and Jack lights a fire.

Then they eat lunch.

34

35

Jack and Jade load their boats.
Then it's time to go.

Jack feels shy.

Jack and Jade wave as they sail away.

# Songbirds

# Tails

Story by Julia Donaldson

Pictures by Carol Liddiment

Series Editor Clare Kirtley

# OXFORD
UNIVERSITY PRESS

# Tips for reading Tails together

This book practises these letter patterns:

> ee  ea  e  y  (all pronounced *ee* as in *three*)
>
> ie  i-e  y  i  (all pronounced *ie* as in *tie*)
>
> ow  o  (all pronounced *oe* as in *toe*)
>
> ai  ay  a-e  a  (all pronounced *ai* as in *train*)

Ask your child to point to these letter patterns and say the sounds (e.g. *ee* as in *three*). Look out for these letter patterns in the story.

Your child might find these words tricky:

> the  to  of  you  all  her  have  do  wants

These words are common, but your child may not be able to sound them out yet. Say the words for your child if they do not know them.

Before you begin, ask your child to read the title. Remind your child to read words they do not recognise by sounding out and blending. Look at the picture together. What do you think this story is about?

When you have finished reading the story, look through it again and:

- Ask your child, *Are tails useful?* (Yes, animals use them in lots of ways: to signal; to help them jump; to help them swim; to help them catch their food; to swish away flies; to show off!)
- Find and read some words on pages 43, 44 and 45 which contain a long *ee* sound (*She, sees, puppy, stumpy, He, happy*). Point to the letter patterns that make the long vowel sound (*e, ee, y, y, e, y*).

Lots of animals have tails.
Tails can be all shapes and sizes.

a zebra's tail

a rat's tail

a whale's tail

a lion's tail

a goat's tail

a crocodile's tail

a skunk's tail

This cat has a long black tail. She waves it when she is cross.

She fluffs it up when she sees a dog.

This kitten likes to chase its tail.

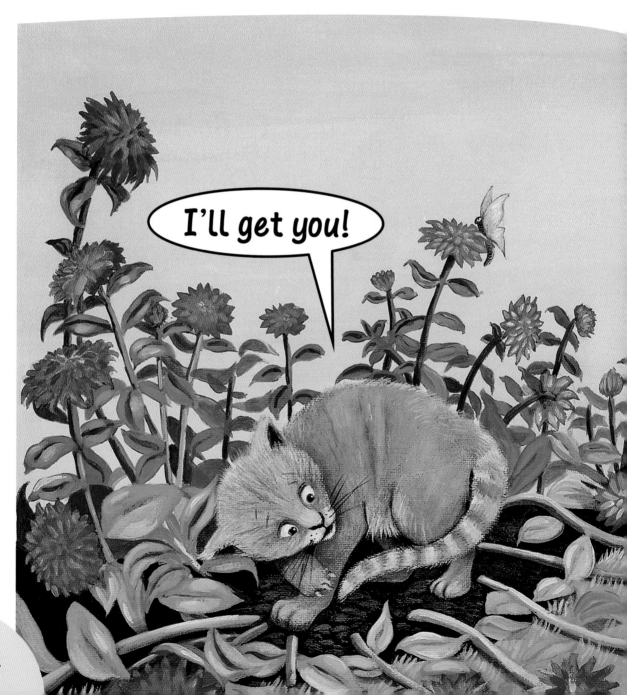

This puppy has a stumpy tail. He wags it when he is happy.

Let's play!

This rabbit has a white bobtail. It flashes when he runs.

That is a signal to run away.

This squirrel has a tail like a brush.
It helps him leap.

This fox has a brush as well. So do her three cubs.

Fish have tails which help them to swim.

This stingray stings fishes with its tail. Then it eats them.

Snakes have scaly tails.

This snake kills the animals it is going to eat, by crushing them.

You won't get away!

This pony has a tail which can swish away flies.

This peacock has an amazing tail. He opens it up like a fan when he wants to show off.

# I wish I had a tail!

# Songbirds

# Pen-Pals

Story by Julia Donaldson
Pictures by Alison Bartlett
Series Editor Clare Kirtley

# OXFORD
## UNIVERSITY PRESS

# Tips for reading Pen-Pals together

This book practises these letter patterns:

> ee  ea  e  y  (all pronounced *ee* as in *three*)
>
> ie  i-e  igh  i  (all pronounced *ie* as in *tie*)
>
> oa  o-e  o  (all pronounced *oe* as in *toe*)
>
> ai  ay  a-e  a  (all pronounced *ai* as in *train*)

Ask your child to point to these letter patterns and say the sounds (e.g. *o-e* as in *jokes*). Look out for these letter patterns in the story.

Your child might find these words tricky:

> of  the  to  you  your  was  are  school  have  one  do  come
>
> love  sneeze  today  can't  goes

These words are common, but your child may not be able to sound them out yet. Say the words for your child if they do not know them.

Before you begin, ask your child to read the title. Remind your child to read words they do not recognise by sounding out and blending. Look at the picture together. What do you think this story is about?

When you have finished reading the story, look through it again and:

- Ask your child, *Did Joan enjoy her stay with Megan? How do you know?* (Yes, because she wrote to Megan that she had had a fab time.)
- Find and read some words on page 71 which contain a long *oe* sound (*Joan, crocodile, home, told, jokes*). Point to the letter patterns that make the long *oe* vowel sound (*oa, o, o-consonant-e, o, o-consonant-e*).

Hi Megan
I am your American pen-pal. My name
is Joan and I am nine. Next May,
twenty kids from my school will be
visiting the UK. Can I stay with you?
Best wishes, Joan

Hi Joan

I am glad we are pen-pals. Yes, you can stay with us in May. I am nine as well, and I like animals. I have a dog. His name is Rex. Have you got a pet?

Best wishes, Megan

Hi Megan

No, I don't have a pet. Dogs make me sneeze. I like playing tennis. I hope you like tennis too.

Joan

Hi Joan
I'm afraid I don't play tennis. I read a lot. Do you like reading?
Megan

Hi Megan

I don't read much but I like TV. My plane gets in at eleven on Friday. Will you meet me?

I hope we will get on.

Joan

Hi Joan
Yes, we can meet the plane. Sorry
but we don't have a TV. We did have
one but it got broken.
See you on Friday!
Megan

## May 1

We met Joan's plane. She is very quiet. I think she is shy.

## May 2

Rex made Joan sneeze. He had to go and stay with Granny.

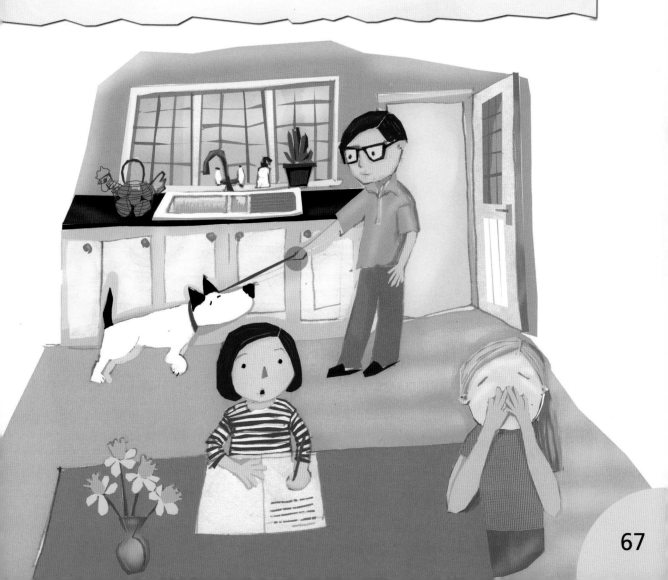

## May 3

Joan was sad today. I think she is missing home.

## May 4

I went swimming with Joan.
It was fun.

## May 5

Joan can play Dad's drums! We sang lots of songs. I like Joan a lot.

## May 6

We went swimming again. Joan made up a game. I was a fish and she was a crocodile. Back home, we told lots of jokes.

Joan and I had a midnight feast!
I will be sad when she goes.

## May 8

Joan had to go home. We got Rex back from Granny's, but I am missing Joan.

Hi Megan

I got home safely. I had such a fab time with you. I can't wait until you come and stay with me next May!

Lots of love

Joan

# Songbirds

# My Cat

Story by Julia Donaldson
Pictures by Barbara Vagnozzi
Series Editor Clare Kirtley

**OXFORD**
UNIVERSITY PRESS

# Tips for reading My Cat together

This book practises these letter patterns:

> ee ea e y (all pronounced *ee* as in *three*)
>
> ie i-e igh i (all pronounced *ie* as in *tie*)
>
> ow o-e o (all pronounced *oe* as in *toe*)
>
> ai ay a-e a (all pronounced *ai* as in *train*)

Ask your child to point to these letter patterns and say the sounds (e.g. *ai* as in *tail*). Look out for these letter patterns in the story.

Your child might find these words tricky:

> to of the out about you head can't

These words are common, but your child may not be able to sound them out yet. Say the words for your child if they do not know them.

Before you begin, ask your child to read the title. Remind your child to read words they do not recognise by sounding out and blending. Look at the picture together. What do you think this story is about?

When you have finished reading the story, look through it again and:

- Ask your child, *Why did the girl find it difficult to write a poem?* (The cat kept disturbing her.)
- Find and read two words which rhyme on pages 84 and 85 (*whale, tail*). Point to the letter pattern that makes the long vowel sound in these words (*a-consonant-e, ai*). Find and read some more words in the book which contain a long *ai* sound (*a, again, say, stay*).

I'm going to write a poem.
I find a pot of ink.
I find a pen. I find a pad.
I scratch my head and think.

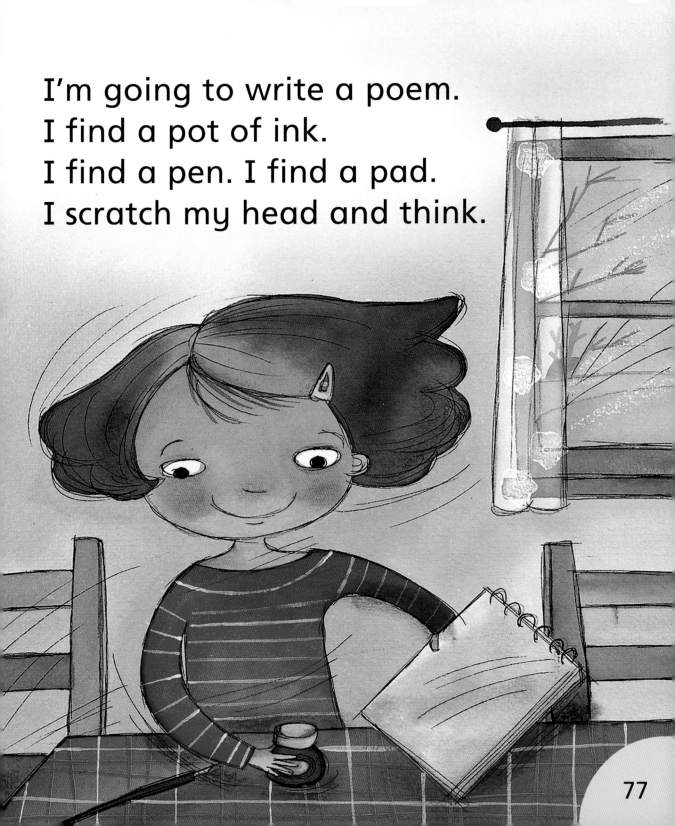

I try to write a poem about my mum and dad.

But then the cat jumps on the desk and sits upon my pad.

I try to write a poem about the
sea and sand.

But then the cat jumps up and
knocks the pen out of my hand.

I try to write a poem
about a bright red rose.

But then the cat jumps up again
and licks me on the nose.

I know! I'll write a poem about a humpback whale.

This time the cat jumps up and knocks the ink off with his tail.

That silly cat keeps bugging me!
I pick him up and say,

"If you won't let me write my poem, then I won't let you stay."

The cat sits on the window sill.
He looks so cold and sad.

I try to write my poem
but I can't help feeling bad.

I suck my pen. I scratch my head.
I think of this and that.

Then suddenly
I've got it!
"I'll write about..."

"My cat!"

# Songbirds

# Tim's Bad Mood

Story by Julia Donaldson
Pictures by Andy Hammond
Series Editor Clare Kirtley

## OXFORD
UNIVERSITY PRESS

# Tips for reading Tim's Bad Mood together

This book practises this letter pattern:

oo

Ask your child to point to this letter pattern and say the sound (e.g. *oo* as in *mood*). Look out for this letter pattern in the story.

Your child might find these words tricky:

the   are   said

These words are common, but your child may not be able to sound them out yet. Say the words for your child if they do not know them.

Before you begin, ask your child to read the title. Remind your child to read words they do not recognise by sounding out and blending. Look at the picture together. What do you think this story is about?

When you have finished reading the story, look through it again and:

- Ask your child, *Was the meat really too dry? How do you know?* (No, Tim was just grumpy about everything because he woke up in a bad mood.)
- Find and read some words with the long vowel sound *oo* on page 98 (*spoon, too, stool*). Point to the letter pattern that makes the long vowel sound in these words. Find and read some more words in the book which contain the letter pattern *oo* (*mood, bedroom, food, boots, pool*). Try and write some on a piece of paper.

Tim Tomkins woke up in a
very bad mood.

108

Then Mum, Dad and Molly said...

# Practise Your Phonics With Julia Donaldson's Songbirds

By the Author of The Gruffalo

## Look out for the other titles in the series ...

**Top Cat and Other Stories**
978-0-19-279296-9

**The Odd Pet and Other Stories**
978-0-19-279297-6

**The Ox and the Yak and Other Stories**
978-0-19-279298-3

**Scrap Rocket and Other Stories**
978-0-19-279299-0

**Where is the Snail? and Other Stories**
978-0-19-279300-3

**Tadpoles and Other Stories**
978-0-19-279301-0

**My Cat and Other Stories**
978-0-19-279302-7

**Leroy and Other Stories**
978-0-19-279303-4

**Where Were You Bert? and Other Stories**
978-0-19-279304-1